A sloth uses its long curved claws to hang from branches.

Poison dart frogs protect themselves with toxins found on their skin.

claws on their front feet and three toes on their back feet.

Emerald tree boas, like all boas, give birth to live young.

Giant otters of the Amazon are the largest otters in the world.

Sloths are good swimmers.

Sloths' fur collects algae, which can give them a greenish tint. This helps them blend into the trees.

Tapirs are related to horses and rhinos.

Many frogs lay eggs in water that collects inside flowers like bromeliads.

Jaguars are the largest cats in North, Central, and South America.

Tamanduas are a type of anteater.

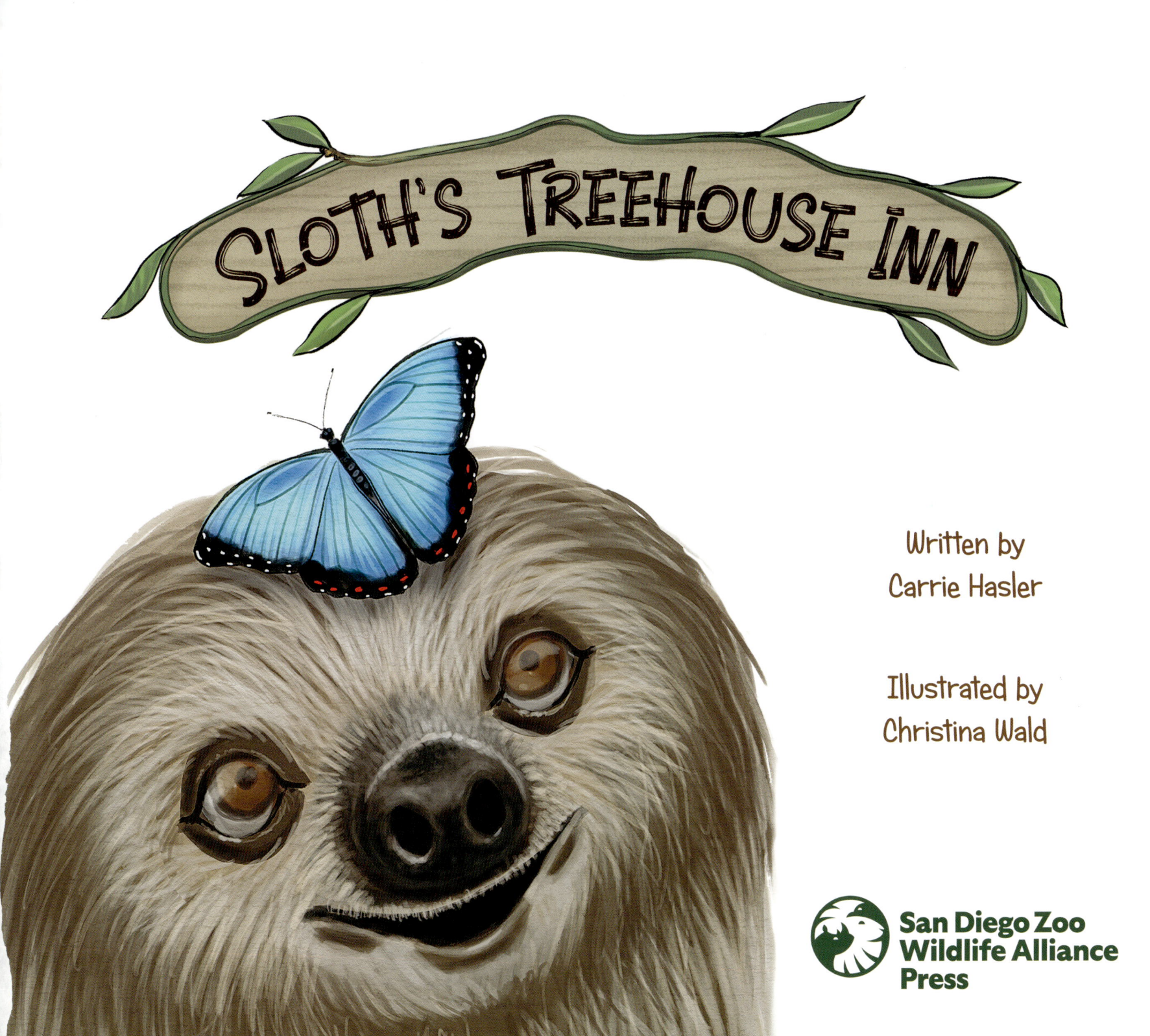

Sloth's Treehouse Inn

Written by
Carrie Hasler

Illustrated by
Christina Wald

San Diego Zoo Wildlife Alliance Press

Sloth's Treehouse Inn was published by San Diego Zoo Wildlife Alliance Press in association with Blue Sneaker Press. Through these publishing efforts, we seek to inspire children and adults to care about wildlife, the natural world, and conservation.

San Diego Zoo Wildlife Alliance is a nonprofit conservation organization that is committed to saving species worldwide by uniting its expertise in animal care and conservation science with its dedication to inspiring a passion for nature. Its vision is a world where all life thrives.

Paul Baribault, President and Chief Executive Officer
Shawn Dixon, Chief Operating Officer
David Miller, Chief Marketing Officer
Georgeanne Irvine, Director of Publishing

San Diego Zoo Wildlife Alliance
P.O. Box 120551
San Diego, CA 92112-0551
sdzwa.org | 619-231-1515

San Diego Zoo Wildlife Alliance's publishing partner is Blue Sneaker Press, an imprint of Southwestern Publishing House, Inc., 2451 Atrium Way, Nashville, TN 37214.

Southwestern Publishing House is a wholly owned subsidiary of Southwestern Family of Companies, Nashville, Tennessee.

Southwestern Publishing House, Inc.
swpublishinghouse.com | 800-358-0560

Christopher G. Capen, President
Kristin Connelly, Managing Editor
Vicky Shea, Art Director

Text and illustrations copyright ©2022 San Diego Zoo Wildlife Alliance

Images courtesy of Shutterstock.com: Veleri, background on endsheets; mlopez, endsheet map; Damsea, 32 top; Martijn Smeets, 32 middle left; guentermanaus, 32 middle right; kungverylucky, 32 bottom left; Kevin Wells Photography, 32 bottom right.

All rights reserved. No part of this book may be reproduced or transmitted in any form or by any means, electronic or mechanical, including photocopying or recording, or by any information retrieval system, without the written permission of the copyright holder.

ISBN: 978-1-943198-13-9 | Library of Congress Control Number: 2021915147

Printed in the Republic of Korea (ROK) | 10 9 8 7 6 5 4 3 2 1

To my mom and dad—
for being my Treehouse Inn when
I've needed it the most.
—CH

To our little blue-green planet
and its lungs, the rainforests. Let's save
the earth before it is too late.
—CW

Nestled deep among the twisting vines and lush leaves of the rainforest was an inn. But not just any ordinary inn. It was the Treehouse Inn, with gnarled branches that stretched to the sky, twisted roots that spread across the forest floor, and hidden places where creatures near and far came to rest.

But, what was most special the about inn was its keeper, a sloth named Santiago.

The Treehouse Inn was a place to relax and go slow, to take long naps and hang around, just like a sloth.

Santiago took great pride in being a caring innkeeper. He managed to find the perfect spot for each of his guests—a long branch for the boa constrictor, a crevice for the jaguar and her cubs, and a nook with its own pool just for the frogs.

Even the smallest and most delicate guest, a blue morpho butterfly chrysalis, was safely placed where the sloth could keep an eye on it. Santiago knew that something magical was happening inside. Hanging like a hammock, he would close his eyes and whisper, "Good night, little butterfly. Take your time."

Everyone who stayed at the Treehouse Inn considered themselves lucky to have such a fine innkeeper.

One afternoon, a pair of loud toucans came squawking in looking for a place to rest for the night. But Santiago didn't think there was enough room.

"The trees in the rainforest are being cut down!" one toucan explained.

"The animals are looking for new homes," the other continued with worry. "They don't have anywhere to go."

No wonder the Treehouse Inn had gotten so crowded.

The lush forest brimming with life was becoming nothing more than a swath of dirt and mud.

Santiago, who was almost always very happy, couldn't help but be very sad.

Every day more animals arrived at the inn—leafcutter ants and tapirs, spider monkeys and macaws, poison dart frogs and giant otters.

Santiago didn't have the heart to turn anyone away. And so, he found room for them all. Soon, every nook and crevice, branch and leaf was filled with creatures at the once quiet Treehouse Inn.

Is there room for us?

Santiago did his best to keep his guests happy. Tea was served every afternoon, pillows were fluffed at night, and games were set out for everyone to enjoy. The sloth was happy to play checkers with anyone who was patient enough to wait while he very s-l-o-w-l-y took his turn.

And every day, Santiago checked on the butterfly chrysalis.

In the evenings, the young ones would gather around while Santiago read bedtime stories. They didn't seem to mind that the sloth was always the first to fall asleep, long before the story was over.

But the guests were starting to squabble. The howler monkeys were awfully loud, and the tamarins were eating all the fruit. They needed more space.

Santiago seemed to always wear a smile, but as he looked at the chrysalis that night, his smile began to fade. "Where will you go when you emerge, my friend?"

The next morning, Santiago woke to a surprise. With wide-eyes, the two friends stared at each other in wonderment. They both stayed still for a very long time, something the sloth happened to be very good at.

Suddenly, the blue morpho butterfly flapped his wings and, in a flash, disappeared through the canopy of the Treehouse Inn.

"Wait! I didn't get to say good-bye!" Santiago called. He slowly began climbing the tree, hoping to see his friend one last time.

When he reached as high as he could go, Santiago's heart sank. So many trees in the rainforest had been cut down.

But, in the distance something was different. People were working together to plant saplings and seeds. Young trees were growing, and smaller plants were sprouting between them.

Was it true? Could the rainforest be returning? Filled with hope, Santiago couldn't wait to tell the others.

As the replanted forest grew taller and began to fill with tangled vines and broad leaves, the animals began checking out of the Treehouse Inn. Santiago pointed them in the direction of their new homes among the young trees. There, the jaguars would have room to roam, the monkeys would have plenty to eat, the tapirs would have places to hide, and the butterflies would have flowers to drink from. Someday soon the rainforest would be as lush as it had once been.

And so, the Treehouse Inn became quiet once again. No more squabbling, no more fighting, no more crowding. There was always a room available, with plenty of space for everyone.

And, even though business was slow, its very fine innkeeper was happy just the way it was.

SAVE THE AMAZON!

The Amazon rainforest is the largest tropical forest in the world. It is home to 430 species of mammals; 40,000 types of plants; 1,300 bird species; 3,000 types of fish; and 2.5 million different species of insects. And, many more species of animals and plants are still waiting to be discovered! Sadly, the Amazon is disappearing very quickly, mostly because of cattle ranching. Large-scale farming and logging are also stripping the land of its trees, and recent fires have devastated the forest. Without trees, animals lose their homes and are disappearing from our planet, too.

But, it's not too late to save the Amazon rainforest!

- San Diego Zoo Wildlife Alliance and its conservation partners are studying animals in the Amazon, such as giant otters and jaguars, to learn more about their behavior and ways to save them.

- Governments, organizations, and communities are working together to create protected areas.

- Farmers are beginning to plant crops that can grow among the trees.

- Selective logging allows a few trees to be harvested without clearing large swaths of rainforest.

- People are replanting the rainforest using special methods such as the muvuca approach, in which a mixture of seeds from a variety of trees and plants are planted, creating a more diverse and dense forest.

If we work together, we can save the amazing Amazon—one of Earth's greatest treasures.

How You Can Help

To learn about conservation and how you can help the San Diego Zoo Wildlife Alliance save species worldwide, visit

support.sdzwa.org

Here are some things to help your local animals and plants that can even make a difference as far away as the Amazon!

1. Tell your friends and family not to buy products made from threatened trees and plants, marine life, or wild animals.

2. Be a scientist! Learn as much as you can about the Amazon and make your own book to share with your family.

3. Help wildlife by building an insect hotel or a bird feeder.

4. Take a nature walk! Identify plants, trees, insects, and animals in your neighborhood and what they need to survive.

5. Be an earth-friendly artist. Use recycled materials when making crafts and use both sides of paper when drawing and coloring.

1. harpy eagle
2. scarlet macaw
3. howler monkey
4. toucans
5. capuchin monkeys
6. toucan
7. howler monkey
8. tamanduas
9. hoatzin
10. Amazon parrot
11. kinkajou
12. emerald tree boa
13. tamarins
14. iguana
15. jaguars
16. sloth
17. poison dart frog
18. tapirs
19. giant anteaters
20. leafcutter ants